κλέφτης
(Thief)

S. A. Timlin

WESTBOW
P R E S S®
A DIVISION OF THOMAS NELSON
& ZONDERVAN

WestBow Press books may be ordered through booksellers or by contacting:

WestBow Press
A Division of Thomas Nelson & Zondervan
1663 Liberty Drive
Bloomington, IN 47403
www.westbowpress.com
1 (866) 928-1240

Because of the dynamic nature of the Internet, any web addresses or
links contained in this book may have changed since publication and
may no longer be valid. The views expressed in this work are solely those
of the author and do not necessarily reflect the views of the publisher,
and the publisher hereby disclaims any responsibility for them.

KJV:
Scripture taken from the King James Version of the Bible.

Gospel of Luke; Isiah

This is a work of fiction. All of the characters, names, incidents,
organizations, and dialogue in this novel are either the products
of the author's imagination or are used fictitiously.

Any people depicted in stock imagery provided by Thinkstock are models,
and such images are being used for illustrative purposes only.
Certain stock imagery © Thinkstock.

ISBN: 978-1-9736-1627-6 (sc)
ISBN: 978-1-9736-1628-3 (e)

Library of Congress Control Number: 2018901014

Print information available on the last page.

WestBow Press rev. date: 02/07/2018

TABLE OF CONTENTS

Introduction vii

About the Author ix

The First century political scene xi

Crucifixion as Punishment xiii

Dedication xv

About The Story.. xvii

One 1

Two 8

Three 11

Four 14

Five 17

Six 20

Seven 23

Eight 27

Nine 29

Ten 33

Eleven 36

Twelve 39

Thirteen 41

Fourteen 45

Fifteen 49

Sixteen... 53

Seventeen 57

Eighteen 60

Nineteen 64

Twenty... 66

Twenty One 68

Twenty Two 71

Twenty Three.. 74

Twenty Four 78

Twenty Five 84

INTRODUCTION

<u>This is a work of fiction</u>. After reading the Gospel of Luke on several occasions, I'd often ask myself "Who was that guy?" In my search through the Bible, I couldn't find any background on the two thieves hung with Christ, so I thought of a story. The Bible references were taken mostly from Luke's gospel. I probably have the story all wrong. I've heard some commentary that the two hung with Christ were rebel insurgents and were trying to lead a revolt against the Romans. Who knows and thank goodness for literary license.

ABOUT THE AUTHOR

I quit my job and moved to Texas. After moving from the Washington DC area to be closer to my parents. I had just arrived in Texas and a short three months later I was found to have a brain tumor. My brain has been operated on four times. After the surgeries and a lot of rehabilitation I was instructed to keep my mind occupied.

After the surgeries, I was left 100% disabled and not able to work. A walker aids simple walking. The surgeries left me without balance. I have double vision so I don't drive. I also use an eye-patch in order to see one image otherwise I see two of everything. Small kids are heard to say to their parents "look a girl pirate!" I have what "they" call emotional liability. These are uncontrolled emotional manifestations in the form of crying that I cannot control. We could be talking about grass growing and the next thing I am crying with tears streaming from my eyes. I can now feel when one is on its way and at least warn the person I am talking to. The only positive note about having one is they don't last long. These things are most inconvenient.

I was placed in a medical induced come for about six weeks in which they inserted a ventilator/breathing tube. My voice was damaged when they removed the breathing tube from my throat, it was determined that my vocal chords had wrapped themselves around the breathing tube and were subsequently damaged when the tube was removed. Although I can speak, my voice sounds like I'm a 10-pack a day smoker. When I get tired, it sounds like I am speaking with a mouthful of marbles.

I hope you enjoy the story but please remember this is a work of fiction.

THE FIRST CENTURY
POLITICAL SCENE

It is believed that Herod the Great was born around 65 BC, became governor of Galilee in 47 BC, and died in 4 BC. Herod the Great built a number of cities, but his principle base was Jerusalem.

In the first century, Israel was ruled by Rome but allowed to worship their God. Rome was fighting threats against it on all sides. It is suggested that after Julius Cesar died General Pompey promoted Herod to be the ruler in Israel. Herod continued his loyalty to Rome after he was in power. I could have this wrong, the important thing to remember is that Herod was ruling.

Herod was a great builder and is known for his supposed reconstruction of the Jewish temple and Temple Mount enlarging it and making it into the most beautiful temple in its time. It was worked on through most of his reign and he managed to rebuild it without affecting the ritual sacrifices. Some of his other achievements include: the rebuilding of water systems for Jerusalem, refurbishing and constructing fortresses such as Masada and creating whole new cities such as

Caesarea. He also instituted relief programs during periods of drought and famine.

Even after all his building and social programs he remained very unpopular with the Jewish people. He was a very cruel leader and had many people executed because of his paranoia. He levied high taxes on his subjects and had many enslaved, imprisoned and executed. Even after all this, Rome still could not bring Israel under control.

CRUCIFIXION AS PUNISHMENT

The Romans did not invent crucifixion but they perfected its use. In this current day and age, it is still used. There are many excruciating effects of crucifixion and it was perfected so that no one could survive. As the body sinks down after being nailed and affixed, with more weight on the nails in the wrists and feet, excruciating pain is felt in the fingers and up the arms. Major nerve endings run along the arms and legs so when the body tries to ease itself searing pain shoots to the brain.

When I look at images of Christ nailed to the cross, it amazes me at how antiseptic they are. The nails used were estimated to be at least five to seven inches long and about a half-inch wide or wider. They had to be capable of holding the weight of a human body. I have also read that sometimes ropes were used to help hold the body in addition to using nails. A modern day small picture nail would not work and would pull the bones and tissues free. I hate needles and the thought of a spike being hammered into my hands and feet make me weak.

Breathing also becomes very difficult. After many hours of excruciating agony, cramps throughout the body would begin. Cramps would incapacitate the sufferer by causing pain when one tried to push oneself up with their legs. The ribcage would not react properly, you could take a breath but exhaling would be extremely painful causing the carbon dioxide level to increase and lead to suffocation.

In order to speed death up, the Romans employed crurifracture. The leg bones would be broken. This would be done using a club or some heavy type of instrument. This stopped the hanging people from raising themselves up causing a more rapid suffocation.

DEDICATION

To My Heavenly Father and Savior, who forgives
EVERYTHING – just ask:

Lord, Jesus
I am a sinner – but you came to save
Lord, Jesus – Save me.
To My Earthly Parents

ABOUT THE STORY

This is a story about forgiveness and chances. Several times our main character John plays witness to the miracles that Jesus accomplished and each time our character chose to turn away in following Jesus only to participate in a short lived activity that offered no promise. One thing you can take from Luke's scripture reference is that it shows that it is never too late to seek and ask for forgiveness. Our thief was facing death when he acknowledged his sin and asked Jesus for forgiveness.

The story tells of John making lifelong bad decisions that eventually end up with him found guilty and crucified. It's a good thing that God gives us chance after chance. At no time this side of life is it ever too late to call out to him.

Imagine this, you've died and are being led down a long hall. You stop in front of a door that is then opened before you. You are guided inside. Beyond the door are hundreds of filing cabinets. The room is filled from floor to ceiling and all sides. You are led to stand before a cabinet and a drawer is pulled open. A file is drawn out and is opened before you. You are now asked to explain what is shown. You are embarrassed, your breath becomes shallow, you feel your heart pounding and you begin to sweat. The individual standing next to you waits patiently for you to explain what you see. You try to form words but you are unable. Nothing you think of will explain what you see in your file.

Your face becomes hot with shame. These folders contain every thought, word or action you did on a particular day since the day you were born. Several times the figure presents you with your files and the process is repeated all with the same outcome. For some of us, we don't want anyone to see our files.

After you have failed to state your case you are led out of the room. You are surrounded by bright beautiful light. You look toward your right and a warm breeze ripples your hair. People are walking arm-in-arm and smiling. Others are walking and singing.

You see several people sitting in groups and it appears listening to talking, standing figures. You notice a river of crystal clear water the breeze is making ripples on the surface. You see beautiful trees and flowers in every conceivable color. You think you have imagined what you see next only to realize that it is very real. A giant creature walks next to a small child and the child is holding on to the creature's great mane. Both the creature and child quickly make their way to the clear water.

An incredible peace and joy overtake you. You never want to leave this place. The figure you follow has claimed your attention to once again follow him. He leads you toward a gate. This is no ordinary gate; it is an ugly gate, in fact a hideous gate it has no end, top, or bottom. Looking through the rails you see only darkness. The other side of this gate is utter darkness no light just complete blackness.

As you approach you hear screams of terror, and heat begins to surround you. As you approach, you become frightened. Terror grips you. The closer you get it becomes more difficult to breath. You struggle for air and it becomes hotter and the screams become louder.

Nothing has prepared you for the terror that awaits you on the other side of this gate. You begin to turn away to run back towards the beautiful clear water only to be led towards the gate. You lose all strength and stumble as the figure opens the gate and waves you through. You try to resist but your attempts are fruitless. You grab hold of the rails but unseen hands grab your legs and tear you free. Turning slowly you scream. You tell the figure you want to join the others and are told you cannot. You ask why and are told, "I never knew you." After passing through the gate the doors shut with a loud reverberating echo. Now your real terror begins.

Jesus is already aware of your every thought, word or action ever since the moment you were born. Now, it's just a matter of you voicing them to him. Be as detailed as you want. I've heard from the PC crowd that as a Christian we are being exclusive. It's really quite the opposite. Christianity is OPEN to everyone. By NOT choosing to have your sins forgiven you make it exclusive.

Jesus died for ALL sins and for each and every one of us no matter what we have or haven't done. Jesus died for our past, present and future sins.

> Lord, Jesus
> I am a sinner – but you came to save
> Lord, Jesus – Save me.

Our character lived through the most incredible moment in history, and yet he turned away at each opportunity to follow another path. He was given a final opportunity while dying on a cross to seek forgiveness, which he received. Even if you were the only person alive Jesus would have died a horrible death just so that you could be with him in heaven. There are many religions that point you to God but only one leads you to him, and yes, Jesus is the only way. What other religion had someone die for you?

Maybe you feel a passion for stopping intolerance and hate. Maybe your passion is to volunteer at the local food pantry or shelter, or maybe you want to save the animals. Maybe you feel the need to save the planet through anti-global warming or pollution controls. Were you baptized? Maybe you are against any type of violence against people. These are all respectable actions but they are just that – acts and they do nothing to get you into heaven.

I have a question for all the good people. Have you ever taken a paper clip, pen, or sticky note from your employer, maybe some postage, an envelope, or maybe some paper? How about some sugar packets for your tea/coffee? If you answered yes, then you have stolen from your employer. Do you still consider yourself a good person?

Was someone you knew murdered? Do you hate someone enough that you wish they were dead? Consider this. You are driving in your car, happily singing along to a song on the radio and suddenly another vehicle cuts you off and almost causes you to drive off the road. You yell and scream obscenities and maybe even wish that person were dead. In your heart you have just killed that person.

We have all been part of this. It is these types of actions (and others) that Jesus came and died for us. We are all guilty of sin, great and small, no matter what we consider good we are all guilty.

Jesus was very clear in describing a very real hell. He doesn't want anyone to go there, it was made specifically for the devil and his followers that's how terrible it is. The devil is very clever in making us believe that things aren't that bad and that hell is not that bad a place. Do not let another minute go by believing this.

On the contrary, hell is a terrible place full of constant and never-ending terror and torment. Heaven is going to be the best you can imagine and conversely hell will be the worst. We are unable to even come close to imaging either.

✝

ONE

I was born in the first century and by the time I am 30 I will be dead – courtesy of a Roman crucifixion.

Hello, I am John. Let me tell you my story.

I am standing on a small outcropping of rocks. I look along the dusty road in both directions. The wind stirs up little swirls of dust on the ground before me. I notice several of my neighbor friends playing and running. These are mostly girls since most of the boys were killed during King Herod's reign many years ago. There are a few older boys but most have just recently moved to our village.

They call me John. I was born in the first century. We are not rich, we are not descended from royalty and my father has to provide for us, he is a shepherd. I have three older sisters and one older brother. I have several younger brothers and sisters. My older sisters survived the reign of Herod the Great. And since he was dead long before my brother was born all my siblings were out of danger of being executed.

Although successful in politics, Herod was not successful in his private life. He married ten wives. He loved one of his wives very much but suspected her of being unfaithful and had her executed. He also had a mother-in-law executed as well as two sons. He had numerous members of his family executed on account of his paranoia. He dealt ruthlessly with suspected rivals and troublemakers by killing them. Upon his own death, Herod had several members of the Jewish community executed so that there would be sorrow and weeping at the time of his death.

From most of the accounts I have heard, Herod was a disaster at politics but was a successful builder and he began many building projects prior to his death. As I look out over the hills I can see several of the building projects King Herod started. There is a flurry of activity around them. From this distance the people look like little ants scurrying about. I can see people carrying buckets and moving about and causing dust clouds to stir up as they walk. Those playing behind me are squealing and laughter is heard all around. Day-to-day life moves on as people make their way to street vendors and the market.

In the upper part of the city lives a wealthy merchant and his family. He owns the village market and charges rent to those who want to sell their goods. My mother often sends me to the market for various items. This wealthy merchant is Abdon's father. I have only interacted with Abdon's father a few times, but I have spoken to his mother on numerous occasions. Abdon is my friend and is slightly older than me but not by many days.

According to my mother, a few days before my birth, another neighbor is preparing for the birth of her next child. Finally she gives birth. This birth was more difficult than the rest. Several of the village women were on hand to help with this birth. It took over a day to finally bring the baby into the world. He is named Abdon; he and I will become lifelong friends and we will end up dying together.

My early life was very uneventful. I can recall nothing that would indicate my ending up crucified. As a small child my actions were common for a boy during my time. Getting into small troubles, I would often find myself having to explain to my father what had transpired. Being under the ever-watchful eye of Rome we were limited in what trouble we could do. This limited our troublemaking but we still found a way.

The First Century found Jerusalem under Roman rule. We abided by Roman rules, and we never had any problems. For the most part, my family lived a very ordinary existence. My father would attend to his shepherding duties and my mother would tend to the house and kids. I am a Jewish male and I will grow up studying and receiving my education in our local Synagogue along with the other boys in my village.

My father is able to provide us a good life and taught us right from wrong. For all of us and at the time of my birth and my adult life he is working as a shepherd. After taking the male children in our household to study at the Synagogue, he would have us follow him and learn about shepherding and the many facets of raising and care of sheep and goats.

We live in a modest house, which has a few windows, a proper door and a roof top area where we sometimes sleep when it gets too hot. For a house located in the lower part of the city, our house was better than most. My friend Abdon lives in the upper city. His home has real marble and tile inside. His drinking water comes from a private well located inside his house and his family does not have to share their water with the rest of the town. His dad is a wealthy merchant and owns the local market place. His father charges the merchants rent of the stalls to sell their items. Abdon has household servants to run his errands and do common household chores. After I do my chores for the day I usually find Abdon at his home waiting for me.

All of my siblings were required to do their part in the household and only afterwards allowed to play. My designated chore was to collect firewood daily. Our home life is a happy one; there were a number of neighbor kids to occupy our time and play. We did a lot of play since the only education I received was in my trips to Synagogue and the reading of the law scrolls and helping my dad in the fields.

My friend Abdon and I met while attending the local Synagogue. We became fast friends. When you attend our particular Synagogue the older men sit toward the front while you progressively get to the younger males the further back you go. The women have their own section separate from the men. I remember on a particularly warm day, the heat was oppressive inside the Synagogue and many inside couldn't wait till the lessons were over to escape the stifling air inside. Abdon had just sat down next to me while his father made his way up closer to the front. After several moments of what seemed like an eternity, I happened to glance at Abdon out of the corner of my eye at his hand, which was clasped over his mouth.

After a short time, what sounded like a sheep's bleating escaped from his mouth. He erupted into fits of laughter that caught me up into laughing as well. After several hard looks from the older men and elders of the Synagogue we quieted down and the lesson resumed only hearing another sheep's blast erupt inside the quiet Synagogue a few moments later. This time we were laughing so hard the tears were streaming from our eyes. Both our fathers escorted us from the Synagogue. Abdon's father grabbed his arm and led him towards the market. My father led me toward the hills. Outside we attempted to quiet down but couldn't. This incident effectively shutdown any more lessons for the day and after a short while members of the Synagogue emerged. Abdon and I would meet at the Synagogue several more times and would develop our friendship over the course of several years.

Our other neighbor also had a son, but he was fond of staying in the temple and discussing the law with the elders. Mary's son is often called upon to read from the scrolls. For one so young, he has the ability to discern the more difficult teachings and often the Pharisees and Sadducees sit in wonder at his discernment of the old teachings. He has the ability to teach and translate the teachings so they make sense to us. I have noticed several of the Synagogue elders whispering with excited hand gestures. Many would mutter under their breath and many had angry looks when they would hear him speak and translate some verse and especially when he would translate the verse into something contrary to what they taught. I remember feeling amazed at this especially since he was so young, I would sit in amazement at how he could know such things. In my heart I think the elders of the Synagogue do not like him. I see the way they whisper and point when he is not facing them.

When my dad takes me to Synagogue, we usually spend the better part of our mornings sitting and listening to the old teachings and law. I loved to sit and hear the old stories. I remember sitting for hours listening to the old stories of Noah, Abraham, and Moses. Abdon would try to move me away from listening but I would shush him.

My mom didn't particularly care for my friend Abdon. She was always trying to get me to play with Mary's son. As my mom put it Abdon was only going to get me into trouble. As I look back she was right.

One day I invited Abdon to eat with us. As my mother and sisters set the meal before us, Abdon reaches in, takes food, and begins to eat. My mother suggests that we eat after we say our thanks and pray. Abdon ignores her and continues to eat. My mother looks to me as if I should say something to him. I sit and remain quiet.

Abdon was the only boy in his family but had older and younger sisters. I guess his parents stopped hoping for another son after him. He often got away with pranks and other situations that others would be reprimanded for trying. Abdon's family was wealthy in comparison to ours – his dad was a market owner. Abdon never lacked for anything; being a merchant's son enabled them to have servants to gather firewood among other things. Abdon's household had several servants. It seemed each area of their house was set with a certain number of servants. The kitchen, living, bathing, and sleeping quarters each had its own servant. Once during a midday meal, the table servant had set out fruit to be eaten with the meal. Abdon was very hungry on this day and had taken a bite from a piece of fruit and put it back on the pile. Abdon's father had seen the piece of fruit with the bite taken out and promptly had the servant severely beaten. The servant had pleaded for himself but Abdon's father would not listen to his pleas. Abdon remained silent.

Many of the house servants stay away from Abdon. He would often yell at them and strike them for what seemed to me a slight offense. I can remember seeing bruises on the arms and faces of the servants. They would not look at Abdon except when directly spoken to.

T W O

Hello, I am Abdon.

You should hear my side of the story. Like John said, I am the only boy from a litter of girls. I say litter because it seems my parents kept trying for boys. I ended up as a result, lucky me. No other boys were born to my parents and only a few girls after me. My mother often showed her love towards me by her tone and the back of her hand. I remember several times the sting of my mother's hand as it struck my face and the heat that my face felt for what seemed like hours after she struck me. I remember experiencing several instances when my mother would focus her special affection on me. I do not recall seeing my sisters experiencing her special attention.

My father often excluded the girls from our outings and he focused much of his attention on me. My father owns the village market. I remember him taking me to collect the monthly rent from the local stall owners. On one of our collections a shop seller did not have quite enough money. This made my father extremely irate. As he yelled at the seller, foam collected in the corners of his mouth and would spray the seller in his face. The shop seller was extremely frightened and I remember feeling excited, warm and glowing during the exchange. The man's frightened face almost made me laugh. He was so scared. Several of the other tenants prepared their rent money and quickly gave it to my father when we stopped in front of their stalls. I remember thinking there was a lot of money collected during this time. We wanted for nothing; if my father saw something of particular interest from the market he would often bring it home to us.

As a small boy, I remember being taken to the local Synagogue to get an education like all Jewish boys of my day. It was there that I met John. After Synagogue, John and I would escape the hot, dusty and confining inner Synagogue room to find better games outside before we had to return to our homes.

I met John one hot day in the Synagogue. The lesson wasn't particularly inspiring but not many of them were. Anyway, I sat next to this skinny kid; I was so bored I began to make noises. I was able to make a few before I was so rudely stopped by the elders. After being led outside with John we decided to see what the Synagogue sellers were selling. I was still bored and told John to stand watch next to one particular merchant who was selling birds. I unlatched the cage. There were just a couple of cages so I unlatched the others as well. By the time the birds started to escape John and I were quietly sitting on the stairs watching the commotion.

The bird sellers ran to their stalls and tried to latch the cages before the remaining birds escaped. Their attempts were unsuccessful. By the time the bird sellers noticed the escaping birds and the empty cages, the feathered flock had made their escape.

Shortly after this episode our fathers came out of the Synagogue and collected us to take us away. We were each asked if we knew what happened but we glanced at each other and denied knowledge of the bird escape. My father gave me a knowing look, grabbed my arm and we made our way home.

On another particularly hot and rainy day, a type of day that limited us to staying occupied at home. Both John and I stayed at our respective homes. My sister and I stayed upstairs. During the course of one game, which we were playing with glassy beads, she got me so mad I picked up a rock and began to strike her with it. Her cries and screams only made me want to keep hitting her. She clasped her head and ran out of the room soon to return with a cloth pressed against her head. She turned angry eyes towards me. An inner warmth reached down into my belly as I contemplated the results of my action. And I smiled.

It is only when my sister really began to make her screams heard that my mother ran into the room and broke up the fight. I remember this was a day that I received more focused attention from my mother. She did not want to hear my side. During dinner that night, my parents discussed the rock incident and my father told my mother that boys played and behaved differently than girls and not to go to extremes when settling matters. I remember my mother looking at me with very real anger. I could almost feel her hand making its way across my face. After this, my mother almost left me alone, and her special attentions almost stopped.

THREE

This is John again. As a shepherd's son, my father and I had access to the village pens and land. My father would drive the flocks to different areas in order to feed and breed them. One day Abdon thought it would be fun to disguise the flock; he did this by applying a thick coat of mud to the entire herd thereby disguising the males and females from one another. It wasn't until you got up close that you could distinguish the males from the females. Afterwards we ran and hid behind some rocks to see the fruits of our efforts. After a little while the owner came by, looked around and scratched his head in wonder of this. We laughed very hard. I think hearing our laughter helped the owner discover my conspiracy in the matter. I was the one who ended up having to wipe and brush the mud off of them. This was just another of many of our exploits and would culminate to my death.

The day is hot and the sun is at its highest point in the sky. I am sitting on the side of the hill, helping my father tend to a small flock. Since our pens are located inside the city walls most of the predators remain on the outside. Occasionally you will hear of the death of an animal. But I am tending this flock and there shouldn't be any problems. The sweat is beading on my forehead and drops are beginning to run down my back in between my shoulder blades. There isn't any shade and no matter what I do I can't get cool. My small flock seems impervious to the heat and continues to graze; they ignore the buzzing flies that swarm around them. I stand up to stretch and see my friend heading my way. I yell to him and he makes his way over to me. He asks me how long I'll be in the fields. I tell him my dad didn't tell me but to watch the flock until he returns. Abdon and I sit for a while under the hot sun. I open the sack my mother gave me. Inside there is a small amount of bread, nuts and fruit to eat. I share what I have with Abdon. After our meal, Abdon begins tossing pebbles into the air. He seems bored. We start chatting and he begins asking me about the strength of the pens. I explain to him that they are sturdy and are made from wood and large rocks. After a while Abdon begins to talk out loud about how safe he thinks the flock would be if left on their own. He voices that because the pens are strong and we are inside the city walls the herd is safe. I tell him that my father sternly instructed me to stay with them. Abdon again argues that because of the structures of the pens and the height of the rails that they would be safe and wouldn't it be fun to go play in the river to cool off.

The river is just a short walk down the hill and looking back up we could see the flock grazing. Soon we were making our way toward the cool water. We took off our outer garments and made our way into the river. I do not know how long we stayed but a lone figure was making its way to us. Shortly I could make out the image of my father. He did not look happy. Soon he was upon us and was pulling me out of the water. He instructed Abdon to go home. Forcefully my father began to drag me up the hill. I didn't notice too much on the way back up the hill. The bleating and other outside noises were mysteriously quiet. It was then that I noticed a brown discoloration on the ground. In a few more steps I noticed what appeared to be wisps of fur. I kept walking only to discover a lifeless member of my flock. It was then that our journey stopped. I have never seen my father so angry. On this day I received the only beating that my father ever gave me.

✝

FOUR

It was a warm day out and I was making my way to Abdon's house. I spotted him sitting in a field. I make my way over to him. He doesn't hear me. His shoulders are hunched over. I come up behind him and glance over his shoulder. His lap is full of flies. These aren't normal flies but flies without their wings. I ask him what he plans on doing with them and he has a gleam in his eyes and tells me to follow him. He leads me to a small outcropping of rocks and shrubs and there he shows me a rather large spider web. I notice a big hairy spider sitting on a corner of its web. It is the size of my thumb. Abdon begins to drop his collection of wingless flies into the web. Abdon claps his hands and laughs when he sees the spider run to its victim and begins to spray its glistening web around the fly. The wingless fly try valiantly to escape the spider but to no success. The spider will save its trophy for later when it is good and hungry. I remember looking at Abdon and noticing the gleam in his eyes. Soon watching the spider loses its attraction for Abdon and we make our way to other pursuits.

On several occasions I would notice small purple bruises on Abdon's arms. Sometimes they would be bright purple and other times they would be yellow and brown and almost gone as if they had been there for a while but were going away. I asked him one time about it and he became very angry with me. Since then when I notice them I remain silent.

To keep me out of Abdon's reach and help out around our home sometimes my mother will lend me out to our neighbors to help with whatever they need help with. Abdon gets pretty upset when this happens because it puts a kink into his daily plans for mayhem. Today I am helping to reinforce livestock pens. After several long hours, I make my way home but get intercepted by Abdon who succeeds in spiriting me away to cause some trouble.

As I finish eating our morning meal and head out to do my chores for the day, Abdon meets me. He points to a rather large stack of wood and tells me that today the wood has been gathered and we can just head off to play. I didn't ask him where or how he obtained such a large stack of wood but was thankful I did not have to worry about the day's chore. It was about a week later that my parents discovered how I obtained the wood. After discovery, I was made to repair my neighbor's rooftop.

Today I am helping our neighbor fix his pens. For some reason his pens have been taken down. I don't anticipate it taking very long and I may be able to salvage the afternoon. As I finish, I see Abdon leaning against a fence post. I make my way over to him. We discuss our plans for the afternoon. Somehow our conversation makes its way to how the pens became absent. I comment out loud that I sure wish the bad karma would stop since it makes me have to restore whatever has been broken and it is very inconvenient to have to give up my day to fix the problem. Abdon does not comment.

For some reason my mother has not lent me out recently. I guess this is a good thing. Maybe my karma has improved but between you, me, and the goats, I think that my comments spoken out loud have penetrated deeply into the mindset of my friend and hopefully I won't be lent out anymore.

It is the Sabbath and the market is closed for the day. Abdon has us searching for small earthen bowls or jugs. He likes the sound they make when they break. After securing a small stash we stand on top of a small outcropping of rocks and throw the small vessels and watch them break. The next day, I am made to go to the potters shed to make replacements for the ones we broke.

FIVE

John is helping a family friend today. I do wish his parents would stop lending him out. I have things to do and his absence makes it harder for me to get what I want done. I am excited. I have found a new purpose. I have taken to helping the Roman guards on crucifixion hill. They have tasked me with collecting the unused nails after they have used what they needed on the condemned. I am biding my time until they allow me to use the hammer. I work especially hard and have decided that if I do my best the day will come when they will allow me to hammer the nails. I can't wait for this; the Romans have perfected this form of punishment. They have perfected the most slow, tortuous and agonizing way to death imaginable. It's a hideous way to die but I enjoy watching it. It seems they have been using this form of punishment for years.

I am practicing my craft. I have taken to practicing on the local animal population. At first trying to catch mice and rats proved almost useless. Trying to affix their little legs proved fruitless. My hunt for larger animals has provided a much better supply of test subjects.

I remember a neighbor telling me his beloved dog was found nailed to a board. I almost laughed, I mean the look on his face with tears barely contained almost made me laugh out loud, I mean really. It was just a dog.

After exhausting my supply of test subjects I feel I am ready to try my hand on the real thing. I am excited and look forward to discussing my readiness with the Roman guards assigned to crucifixion hill.

After several months and proving myself worthy, the Roman guards have taught me how to properly secure the feet of the condemned. I remember my first attempt. After the guard instructed me in the proper way to hold the nail so that the maximum impact can be made I was allowed to make a strike. It ended badly with the force of the hammer simply striking the leg. After a failed second and third attempt I finally found success. I remember the sound with each strike. My euphoria was cut short due to the screams of the condemned man. I do wish they would be quiet.

Prior to my mastery of the nail, I would take practice hits on anything with wooden nails. These attempts proved futile since they would often break apart and splinter. The result would elicit a response from those being hit. It was good practice for me. It did allow me to become more proficient and accurate with each attempt. The guards would allow me to hone my practice since one day soon I would be the lucky one to hammer in the nails.

Today I will be given my own supply of nails. The guards have told me that I am an apt pupil and that I take my task very seriously. After a few failed attempts and with a Roman guard supervising me, I finally find success. During my learning stage I had to ignore the screams of those who were lucky enough to be my test subjects. My task required my extreme concentration. It was hard to concentrate when the subject would yell out. It's quite a nuisance really. After a few tries, I would ignore the cries and screams and would simply focus on the job to be done.

I would make my way to the hill every day. On one day, I was concentrating on my task when the one assigned to me said "I hope you enjoy your task and never have to experience what I am now going through." I said to him that I wouldn't be foolish enough to get caught. And with an exasperated sigh I find my target and hammer home the nail. I do wish those on the cross would be quiet. It would make my job easier if they wouldn't react as they do.

After my task is complete, I make my way to John. I can barely make him out. He has taken to sometimes following his neighbor's son and stopping to listen to him. Frankly I don't see what the attraction is in following him. It annoys me that he gets absorbed into following him. I have to think of creative ways to have John focus his attention on our outings. I cannot begin to express my frustration with John when I have to physically drag him away.

SIX

Our village was smaller than some of the other villages in the region and we all had to share the common well for our drinking and cooking water. Abdon thought it would be fun to see if we could raise the water without a bucket. He did this by collecting small rocks and pebbles and throwing them into the well. His attempts didn't amount to raising the water it only made it unusable. I was again made to clean out the pebbles and rocks.

I remember another incident where Abdon and I came across a house and outside was piled their wood for the day. Abdon thought it would be fun to move the woodpile – so we did – we moved the wood to the end of the fence then ran and hid behind a building to wait and watch. The door soon opened and a woman emerged to get some wood only to discover the wood was more than a few more steps away than the day before.

My mother has entrusted me with money to go to the market to buy beans for the day's meal. While standing at a stall I notice a look on Abdon's face, one that I will come to recognize in the future as not boding well for me. He tells me to stay where I am and to wait for him to return. I lean my back against the stone wall and a small commotion catches my attention. Walking towards me is a man and his arms, legs and head are wrapped. As he gets closer, the merchant from the stall runs out excitedly and embraces the man. The merchant exclaims and gestures wildly and asks the man what happened. The younger man tells his tale. A short time later the man finishes his tale and is led by the older man inside the stall. I am left to wonder if Abdon had a part in the man's tale. According to the man, a fire broke out among several of the merchants in the market to the town north of ours. The young man tried to subdue the blaze only to be engulfed in the fiery blaze himself. It was only by being grabbed by other merchants that he was dragged to safety. Quick-thinking shoppers put out the flames but not before flames burned his arms, legs, and hair. The shoppers were able to splash water on the young man.

After what seemed like hours, Abdon returns with a small silken bag full of beans, he tells me that we are going to use the money my mother gave me to buy beans and use it for something else from the market. He separates the coins and gives me some and he takes the others. I immediately head to the sweet makers stall and begin to buy as many treats as my money will allow. Abdon heads off in search of a blade of some sort. After consuming the sweets, I begin to feel sick and start to hunt for Abdon to tell him I am heading home. I see him at a stall testing a blade.

After our adventure at the market I make my way home. I give the silken bag to my mother who asks me where I got it. I was unaware that the bag was worth more than the beans and even the money she gave me was little when compared to the beans and the silken bag.

SEVEN

Several years have passed and my group of friends has expanded somewhat. Most are boys from the Synagogue where we have been attending for years. Abdon is still running with this group as well. Much to my mother's frustration, I still count Abdon as my closest friend. She continues to try to get me to hang around Mary and Joseph's son but he just wants to hang out in the Synagogue. Mary's son is the only one absent from our group. He would much rather discuss scripture and the law with the elders rather than hang with us.

On one occasion our group is trying to think of something fun to do. We each give our opinion only to be shot down. Abdon provides us with his idea and many in our gang agree that it would be fun. I look back and realize this is the turning point to my present state. Abdon's idea is to hide and wait on the main road and scare the travelers coming to the Synagogue for the feast day and to make a sacrifice. We each take our positions behind rocks and boulders and wait. Soon a traveler is seen making his way down the road. At the opportune time Abdon gives a signal and we all jump out and scream at the unsuspecting man. He screams and begins to run, we all erupt in laughter and tears fall from our eyes. While breaking into a run our victim loses his moneybag and it falls to the ground. Abdon picks it up and counts the gold coins inside. It is a small fortune. Abdon counts the coins and gives us each a share. We all praise Abdon for his imagination.

We continue this form of harassment for a number of years. I suspect for Abdon that at some point this kind of fun loses its appeal. He wants to improve his tactic. During one episode, after we have scared our traveler, and before he runs away, Abdon brandishes a small knife and demands money. The traveler promptly turns over his moneybag and makes his escape. Many in our gang are horrified by this and leave never to hang around us again. Abdon opens the moneybag and divides up its contents. This traveler's bag contained many riches. There were gold coins, rings, and other items.

I am again entrusted with money and told to go pick up a small table my father had ordered from our neighbor Joseph. As I await the table, Mary's son opens the door and steps through, we exchange a few words and he begins to walk down the path. He turns back to face me and asks if I want to go with him. "To where?" I ask, and he says to the Synagogue. I tell him that I am waiting on a table for my parents but maybe next time. He turns around and continues on his way.

I am waiting for Abdon at the Synagogue; we are headed off to cause trouble somewhere I am sure. Our adventures always come as a surprise to me. To pass the time until Abdon arrives, I wait in the Synagogue. Mary's son is there along with a small group of men. Over the years he has really grown into the doctrine; many think he is a prophet or healer. The temple elders again call on Mary's son to read.

He begins to read from Isaiah. His voice carries throughout the room as he reads *"For I am the LORD thy God, the Holy One of Israel, thy Savior"* (Isaiah 43:3) and also *"I, even I, am the LORD; and beside me there is no Savior."* (Isaiah 43:11) (KJV) after a brief pause he reads *"Yet I am the LORD thy God from the land of Egypt, and thou shalt know no god but me: for there is no Savior beside me."* (Hosea 13:4) (KJV) The temple elders scoff at his reading and question him if he thinks that he is God. The inner hall erupts in shouts with the temple elders yelling "blasphemy!" and I watch as several members tear their robes. I am not close enough to hear what was said but I ask one man who was sitting towards the front what has happened. He states that after reading from the sacred scrolls Mary's son claimed to be the savior.

Many of the city's sick and unwell hover and live either inside or near the Synagogue. They ask for food or money for their daily existence. Mary's son is speaking again to this group of people when one of the sick makes his way over and begins to cry out in a loud voice. The small group obscures the sick man and he is lost in a sea of fabric. All of a sudden he emerges from the group and makes his way toward the exit of the Synagogue. I am astounded. Shortly before this man could hardly walk a straight line and now he appears to walk normally without the need of a crutch. On my way to investigate Abdon tells me to hurry and "come on" he has something planned for our day. As I make my way out of the Synagogue I happen to glance back at the small group of men inside the Synagogue and catch Mary's son looking at me.

EIGHT

My father has assigned me to watch a flock for the night. After a full day of tending the flock I get ready to settle in for a long night. I stoke up the fire and pile my stack of wood for when I awaken and need to add fuel to my fire. Tonight is a rather lonely night in that I will be alone. I begin to prepare for a long night of watching the flock as they sleep.

I am preparing my little area and spread my blankets around me. I eat what my mother has prepared for me and I sit and become warm in front of the fire. I place my slingshot and rocks along with my staff along my side and I curl up in front of the fire. The night is very bright and I can see small dots along the hills where my flock has settled themselves. My eyes begin to get heavy and I am soon asleep.

After a number of hours something wakens me. I am unsure; the night sounds seem distant and strange. I am startled to find Abdon standing over me with a rather curious look on his face. He shakes me more awake and sits next to me. He has that look again. The look that I just know is going to get me into trouble.

His plan is simple really. We will switch all flocks while the shepherds sleep. When they wake all flocks will be in different fields. It takes several hours to finish our plan. The plan is truly amazing and not one shepherd was awakened. Abdon and I are exhausted and sweaty. After several hours and several attempts to move the flocks, we finally find success. Each field has new occupants under a different shepherd. We begin to giggle and as we look at each other we clap each other on the back for our success. We are excited and remain awake to watch the outcome of our plan.

The next morning, several of the shepherds are puzzled as to what occurred. As each awakens in his field, his puzzled looks and mutterings can be heard carried on the breeze. I laugh as I notice several shepherds scratching their heads in puzzlement. They went to sleep tending their flocks only to awaken the next day with their flock in someone else's field.

My flock was the only group that escaped. Somehow my father was suspect to what happened and tasked me again with helping his friends switch the flocks back correctly. As I begin what I know will be a long hard task, I notice Abdon is making his way from the scene of the crime and is headed back toward town.

✝

NINE

8 And there were in the same country shepherds abiding in the field, keeping watch over their flock by night. 9 And, lo, the angel of the Lord came upon them, and the glory of the Lord shone round about them: and they were sore afraid. 10 And the angel said unto them, Fear not: for, behold, I bring you good tidings of great joy, which shall be to all people. (Luke 2:8-10) (KJV)

It has been a long and tiring day. Our family sits down to our evening meal. Today is special in that we have gathered as a family to eat. Usually my father and I are at Synagogue or in the fields tending to the flocks. As we eat I notice the sun is hanging low over the horizon. The weather is cool and the daily heat has left for the season. As I pass my gaze back to our meal, my gaze passes over my father and I notice a far away expression has washed over his face. The room becomes quiet and I ask him what his thoughts are. He begins his tale: I was a young man and the night was cold and I remember there were several of us tending to our flocks. We were sitting around our fire and eating. The night sounds were muffled; we heard a cricket chirping nearby, and the sound of the flocks preparing to sleep. The hour had grown late then I remember a great shaking in the ground. We were scared and we huddled together; the night sky rent open and a bright light opened up the blackness of the night over our heads it was as if the sky broke open and the sun had come out over us. The other hills remained black and the light only affected our hill. All the flocks remained calm and seemed to ignore the light.

There appeared in the sky people as if floating on air. There were many of these beings. Our group huddled closer together. A loud voice told us not to be afraid. These people were all singing and joyous and told us that a baby had been born this night that would deliver us. We were too afraid to consider what was told to us. Much more was said but I cannot recall the words I was still very frightened and trying to regain my strength for I was a young man at the time and I had fallen to the ground afraid. As suddenly as these messengers came they were gone. After the sky had knit itself back together a bright star shone over our village and seemed to point the way to where the messengers had indicated the baby was born. Several of the older men decided to investigate the beam of light that seemed to point downward. A few others and myself were left to tend the flocks and watch for beasts. We were too afraid to leave our fire. It seemed like hours had passed and the group of men finally returned. We asked about the baby and we were told that he lay in a manger and the parents were close to him but no one else attended him. After the group returned, we surrounded them and pressed them for more details. One shepherd in particular was more affected by the baby than the others. The group that had gone to discover what was at the end of the star started as one to speak. But there were many different fantastic stories. I asked my father whatever had become of the baby and he indicated that he thought maybe he died because at the time, King Herod had ordered a great slaughter of baby boys up to the age of two and he couldn't believe that this baby was able to make it to safety. I would later find out the truth behind the story.

My mother told us that father came back from that night and he was changed. His temper no longer flared when a small trouble arose. She added to his story and told us of a great decree by King Herod. He ordered the slaughter of children under the age of two. His decree passed over our family since my sisters were only born to my parents. After our meal my siblings and I are finishing up our daily chores when my father burst into our house. He excitedly searches around the house and finds my mother upstairs with several of my sisters. I hear screams and several shrieks then my father comes running down the stairs with a large knife in his hand. He rushes out the door. I ask my mother what had excited my father so much. She told me my father and several others were searching for the person who had sawed off the horns to several of their flock.

I found this rather funny but had to cover my mouth and turn my face away or else I would not be able to stop the laughter that threatened to burst from me. The sight of several sheep, goats, rams and the flock missing their horns shocked me but for some reason did not surprise me. However; it did threaten a very large burst of laughter as well as a huge smile from me. My thoughts immediately leapt to where Abdon had been this day and it seemed he might have a hand in this episode. After my chores were complete I decided to make my way over to his house and get to the real story.

Nothing of any importance happens for a while. In fact, my existence to this point has been very mundane. I continue to go to the Synagogue for my daily instruction. I continue to hang out with my friend Abdon, and yes he continues to get me into trouble. Nothing can really deter me from hanging out with him; we just have too much fun when we hang out together. I do sometimes wonder why I am the one to make restitution when some of his ideas require the destruction of an item.

TEN

Several more years have passed and still nothing of great importance happens. My family is heading to the next town over near Cana for a wedding. I am not sure if it is my cousin or an aunt or uncle. I will find out when we get there. The women run ahead to do whatever it is that they do and my father and I slowly make our way to the home. We come up to the house and it is full of activity. I see my mother and sisters inside helping to prepare the feast.

A rather large group has gathered outside to make merry. I see several friends and relatives I haven't seen in a while. I make my way over to this group. There is excited chatter and our group gets caught up over what has transpired since the last time they were together. It will be a long day. We will feast after the married couple is presented to the group. There are many people at this gathering and it appears that the whole village has turned out for the party. As I look around I notice Mary's son with a small group of friends.

Suddenly the young couple appears and is presented to the group. Finally we can eat. I am at an age that I can sit with the men, as I take my seat I see several of my father's friends. The tables are weighed down with many yummy dishes and jugs of wine. The guests begin to eat and drink and there is much singing and merriment.

After several hours the head servant approaches my mother. Excited whispers are exchanged. A look of concern crosses my mother's face. Mary notices the look and rushes to my mother's side. There is a flurry of words and gestures between them and the servants. Soon Mary's son approaches and appears to manage the situation. After the commotion is settled, several of my father's friends begin to reminisce about their earlier days. I enjoy hearing these tales. One friend in particular reminds my father about a night long ago and tells my father that the baby did in fact make it to safety and in fact that baby is Mary's son.

Several people at our table inquire about the story and both my father and his friend recount the story of their being on top of the hills many years ago. It appears both have found out what happened to the baby. It seems the family had run to Egypt to escape the decree by King Herod to slaughter the baby boys in the land. They had lived in Egypt for a short while before returning to our village. It is where they now live. Joseph is very handy with wood and tools and Mary's son has grown to be a popular teacher. In fact many tell of his ability to work many signs and miracles. The Synagogue priests are jealous not only of his knowledge and understanding of the ancient texts but his ability to ease the suffering of those in need and his ability to work wonders. The elders are often mad when he heals someone; these healings are mostly done on the Sabbath, which greatly angers the temple elders.

The festivities continue well into the night. After much of the food and wine is consumed we make our way home. The next day will be upon us and there will be much to do.

ELEVEN

I am a bit older now. My days are filled with learning in the temple and then learning about tending flocks from my dad. I still associate with my friend Abdon and yes I still get into small scrapes now and then. Abdon has pretty much left the daily instruction at our local temple. I still attend with my father and brothers. Mary's son has a little bit bigger group of dedicated followers. He has a steady group of about twelve, there are many more but the small group remains unchanged, the others come and go at will and the bigger group fluctuates in size.

The temple is awash in rumors and many of the elders are often seen gesturing wildly. The rumors that are often repeated contain some fantastic stories. Stories such as people who are sick and cannot walk are made whole: several stories have been told of people coming back to life. It is amazing. I often wonder if these stories are true. Mary's son is often found surrounded by the elders after the rest of us have finished our lessons for the day. He sits surrounded by the temple elders and vigorously discusses the law or some other topic. A look of amazement can be seen on the faces surrounding him.

Not all discussions are positive. I have seen and heard several arguments between him and the elders when something is said against the law. Many of the elders get up and cry and some have even ripped their outer garments when something particularly disturbing is said. I try to make my way closer but most times the situation ends about the time I am able to make my way to hear the discussion. It often frustrates me that I am not quick enough. Many of the elders have been heard making evil plans. I could hear bits of their conversation and the words blasphemy and death were carried in the air.

> *17 And it came to pass on a certain day, as he was teaching, that there were Pharisees and doctors of the law sitting by, which were come out of every town of Galilee, and Judaea, and Jerusalem: and the power of the Lord was present to heal them. 18 And, behold, men brought in a bed a man, which was taken with a palsy: and they sought means to bring him in, and to lay him before him. 19 And when they could not find by what way they might bring him in because of the multitude, they went upon the housetop, and let him down through the tiling with his couch into the midst before Jesus. 20 And when he saw their faith, he said unto him, Man, thy sins are forgiven thee. (Luke 5:17-20) (KJV)*

22 But when Jesus perceived their thoughts, he answering said unto them, What reason ye in your hearts? 23 Whether is easier, to say, Thy sins be forgiven thee; or to say, Rise up and walk? 24 But that ye may know that the Son of man hath power upon earth to forgive sins, (he said unto the sick of the palsy,) I say unto thee, Arise, and take up thy couch, and go into thine house. 25 And immediately he rose up before them, and took up that whereon he lay, and departed to his own house, glorifying God. (Luke 5:22-25) (KJV)

I am making my way out of town and happen to pass by a house that has a rather large multitude of people surrounding it. There is great noise coming from those standing outside. Soon I see people on the rooftop and they are quickly removing it. The group stands transfixed to see what would happen next and were surprised to see them lower a hammock with a crippled man inside. I ask one of the men gathered outside what was going on and he said there was a healer inside and they were lowering the crippled man in to be healed. Suddenly there was a commotion and the multitude parted. Looks of wonder and amazement were on the faces of those as the crippled man made his way out of the house. I couldn't believe it; this man was crippled and now could walk. I peered inside the house hoping to catch a glimpse of the healer and saw Mary's son with his group of friends. He turned and I caught his eye glancing at me. He beckons me with a wave of his hand to follow but I yell back "next time!"

TWELVE

¹⁰ And looking round about upon them all,
he said unto the man, Stretch forth thy hand.
And he did so: and his hand was restored
whole as the other. (Luke 6:10) (KJV)

We were all sitting in the Synagogue listening to the daily lesson. The day was warm and the buzzing insects made a soothing sound and drowned out the noise you could hear outside in the courtyard of the Synagogue. A local man who came daily to the Synagogue and had a crippled arm was sitting near the doors. As soon as Mary's son entered, he jumped to his feet and began to cry out and beg him to be healed. Mary's son turned and spoke to the man. Soon after, the man was running from the Synagogue into the courtyard. From his garment only a portion of his arms and legs could be seen. I clearly remember that this man had a left arm that was withered. But as he ran from the Synagogue I caught only a glimpse of his arm and it appeared healed. I wondered in amazement, Mary's son was the only person this man had spoken to and now his arm was healed. If I hadn't seen it I would not have believed it. Then I see Mary's son. I catch his eye and he beckons me with a wave of his hand to follow but I yell "next time!"

THIRTEEN

13 And when the Lord saw her, he had compassion on her, and said unto her, weep not. 14 And he came and touched the bier: and they that bare him stood still. And he said, Young man, I say unto thee, Arise. 15 And he that was dead sat up, and began to speak. And he delivered him to his mother. (Luke 7:13-15) (KJV)

I was making my way to Abdon's house when I encountered a small gathering of people. They were carrying a rather large basket upon which lay a young man and he appeared to be sleeping. I figured he was dead because there were several people following the group and all were weeping. Mary's son and his small group of followers stood to the side of the road in order for the group to pass. Mary's son reached in and whispered something; just as soon as he did the young man sat up surprising everyone. Several people in the crowd screamed, others cried, and others were awestruck and said nothing. An older woman I assumed was the mother of the young man stood beside the basket looking in and began to cry and gesture. After the small procession had passed, Mary's son turned about looking into the crowd and we looked at each other. The group began to make their way up the hill and I turned to make my way to Abdon's house. He beckoned me with a wave of his hand to follow but I yelled back "next time!"

> [16] *Then he took the five loaves and the two fishes, and looking up to heaven, he blessed them, and brake, and gave to the disciples to set before the multitude.* [17] *And they did eat, and were all filled: and there was taken up of fragments that remained to them twelve baskets. (Luke 9:16-17) (KJV)*

I am going to meet up with Abdon on the main road to the city. Along the way I follow a group of people headed to a nearby hill to hear a local preacher speak. I have a few minutes and decide to follow the group. I take my space near the top of the hill in order to hear better and I notice Mary's son ascending the hill. He has his regular group of men in attendance and each of them sits near his feet. As I wait, I look across the distance and see crucifixion hill – at least that is what I call it. I notice a small Roman contingent standing guard under six crucified bodies.

I also notice an individual making his way up crucifixion hill. He stops and looks up to one of the condemned. It appears that words are exchanged between the two. What is said I won't know until later. The shape appears recognizable to me, in fact I think it is Abdon. He is rather obsessed with the ones he meets hanging on crucifixion hill. I see him gesture wildly. He reaches down and grabs a handful of dirt and throws it on the one hanging closest to him. A couple of the guards make their way over to Abdon and point him away. He begins to make his way down the hill.

There is a break in the wind and various noises make their way to where our group sits. We can hear soft whimpers and moans on the breeze. I cannot be certain but I think these are coming from crucifixion hill. Some in our group dart their eyes to the hanging bodies. Sometime in the not too distant future I too will be hanging from a post. But for right now I sit on this mountain.

I turn my focus back to the group I am with on the hill and begin to listen to Mary's Son speak. I am amazed; I have heard him speak on several occasions. I am completely absorbed. He claims the attention of the group as he does when in the Synagogue speaking. We all sit in rapt attention listening to his every word. Although it only feels like minutes have passed it has been several hours and people are leaving to make their way home. Suddenly I am handed a basket that has several roasted fish and warm loaves of bread inside. We are told to take one of each and to pass the basket around our group. I sit in wonder how there appeared so much food. Not only the quantity but also it was roasted and baked perfectly. There are several thousand people sitting on the hill listening and all were able to take a loaf and fish. Even after we have eaten, I look inside the basket and see several fish and loaves remaining.

Abdon has a terrible sense of timing, he finds me and we head off to make mayhem. I ask him where he has been and he confirms my earlier thoughts about seeing him on crucifixion hill. He tells me that he had words with one of the condemned and it would have been worse had not a Roman soldier directed him away. I asked him what had upset him and be begins to tell me. I look in horror as Abdon recounts his story. The one hanging from the cross has made a prediction to Abdon. He states that a few short years from now Abdon will end up where he is and that he would get to experience first-hand what it is like to be nailed to a post. Abdon states that only fools get caught and that the criminal needs to think about his journey after he dies. The criminal again berates Abdon and Abdon grabs small pebbles and dirt and rubs it in the condemned man's open areas. A guard grabs Abdon and turns him away. The episode doesn't appear to affect him.

Abdon went to the hill as usual. We were to meet up later; today he was focused on his task of nailing feet to the cross when a criminal somehow escaped from him. There was a short struggle and Abdon was able to grab hold of one of his legs and secured it to the cross eliciting a scream from the man and creating another short struggle. After some help from the Roman guards Abdon is able to secure the criminal. This criminal then remains stationary while Abdon collects his other leg. I remember Abdon was upset because it caused him to use up more of his inventory. Metal was expensive in our day and we reused everything; they simply melted it down and reformed it.

FOURTEEN

³⁰ And Jesus answering said, A certain *man* went down from Jerusalem to Jericho, and fell among thieves, which stripped him of his raiment, and wounded *him*, and departed, leaving *him* half dead. (Luke 10:30)*(KJV)*

I am sitting on a stone that meets the side of Abdon's house. He told me to meet him here. In talking with him the other day he has promised me that today will be very fun and he 'promises' me that we will not get into any trouble. But a very dark cloud feels like it has settled over me. I cannot help but feel that today will impact me for the rest of my life. All this does nothing to allay my thinking or to make me stop and just head home to where chores and other responsibilities lie.

I can hear someone approaching. It is Abdon. He greets me and we make our way to the main road. I ask him in what direction we are headed and he tells me 'Jericho.'

The day is sunny and warm. Small beads of sweat are running down my back. We have been walking for a number of hours. Suddenly Abdon tells me to hide behind a small grouping of trees. I peer from behind a particularly fat tree and notice a man walking towards us.

The man only makes a few steps past where we are hiding when Abdon jumps out behind him and with a rock hits the man over the head. The man falls to the ground where he remains still. Abdon yells at me to search the man for his moneybag but I tell him I cannot find one.

After being briefly motionless, the man slowly gets to his feet and touches his head. A bewildered look crosses his face and he questions Abdon asking him "Why did you attack me?" A fierce look crosses Abdon's face and the man's question enrages Abdon and he proceeds to attack the man more severely. After several minutes of beating the man Abdon loses his rage and with a look of disgust tells me to collect the man's garments for we are heading home.

We walk home quietly each to his thoughts. I glance at Abdon and notice a slight grin around his mouth. I am confused and somewhat bewildered. Abdon had not told me of his plans.

After walking several hours Abdon turns to me and with glee in his face and voice asks me "wasn't that fun?" I could only stand and look at him while he continues walking. I run to catch up and grab his arm. "Abdon, I did not have fun, in fact we attacked that man for nothing!" "Oh John, what good is practice? We need to practice until we get it right!"

I had no idea what he was talking about. Practice for what? I was left with many more questions during our long walk home. We had just entered our village when Abdon tosses me the man's garments and tells me they are mine. I stand in the middle of the street holding the garments and see drops of red blood. I turn the garments over and notice larger spots of red. The only thought I had at the time was how I was to hide these items.

The unlawfulness of our act did not cross my mind. I look up from the bundle of clothes and see Abdon waving goodbye and yelling at me to come by tomorrow.

> *14 And he was casting out a devil, and it was dumb. And it came to pass, when the devil was gone out, the dumb spake; and the people wondered. (Luke 11:14) (KJV)*

One of Abdon's favorite games was to taunt the sick and unwell of our village. There happened to be a local man that most people stayed away from. He was often seen walking on his hands and knees and speaking in undistinguishable terms. This scared most people, but not Abdon. Abdon would often chase this man throughout the streets. You would often see the man hanging around the Synagogue where people would throw scraps of food to him. One day, Abdon was about to harass this man when he turned around and looked directly at Abdon and told him to STOP! Abdon's look of astonishment brought laughter to the surface. However, when Abdon turned his gaze to me, his look was murderous. I stopped laughing immediately. About a week later I learned that Mary's son had spoken to him and had healed this man.

> *10 And he was teaching in one of the Synagogues on the Sabbath. 11 And, behold, there was a woman, which had a spirit of infirmity*

eighteen years, and was bowed together, and could in no wise lift up herself. ¹² And when Jesus saw her, he called her to him, and said unto her, Woman, thou art loosed from thine infirmity. ¹³ And he laid his hands on her: and immediately she was made straight, and glorified God. (Luke 13:10-13) (KJV)

My father and I are in the Synagogue. We sit with the rest of the men. I am now old enough that I do not have to sit with the boys. The women are designated to sit in a different area. We haven't been sitting for long when an older woman approaches the middle and makes her way to the front where the scrolls are read. She is severely bent over like she is picking something up from the ground. The elders are angry with this woman for disturbing the group and try to get her to go back and sit down. She refuses and continues to make her way to the front of the temple. She is focused and makes her way up front. She stops just short of Mary's son. Mary's son says something to her and she immediately straightens herself upright. The elders of the Synagogue erupt in yelling, some say that she was healed by the devil, some say by magic, however the woman says her praise to God and makes her way out of the Synagogue.

I sit and stare at Mary's son who continues to fix his gaze downward. His glance briefly passes my way but I look elsewhere.

FIFTEEN

¹¹ And he said, A certain man had two sons: ¹² And the younger of them said to his father, Father, give me the portion of goods that falleth to me. And he divided unto them his living. ¹³ And not many days after the younger son gathered all together, and took his journey into a far country, and there wasted his substance with riotous living. ¹⁴ And when he had spent all, there arose a mighty famine in that land; and he began to be in want. ¹⁵ And he went and joined himself to a citizen of that country; and he sent him into his fields to feed swine. ¹⁶ And he would fain have filled his belly with the husks that the swine did eat: and no man gave unto him. ¹⁷ And when he came to himself, he said, How many hired servants of my father's have bread enough and to spare, and I perish with hunger! ¹⁸ I will arise and go to my father, and will say unto him, Father, I have sinned against heaven, and before thee. (Luke 15:11-18) (KJV)

Today I am headed over to a friend's house. I met him while attending our local Synagogue and getting our daily instruction. His family is very wealthy. His father has even more riches than Abdon's father. He has asked his father for his inheritance and plans to move far away. After arriving, I help him pack his few belongings for his journey. We tie his belongings and money chest securely to his donkey. In a few moments he will be on his way. We sit quietly for a moment. The only sounds are those we hear from the village. I begin to ask him what he plans to do when he arrives at his final destination. He informs me that his inheritance should last him many years and it should enable him to live comfortably for the rest of his life. I am curious as to where his father and brother are and why they have not shown up to say goodbye. After a few minutes he bids me farewell and sets off on his journey.

I am concerned for my friend. Some say there is want coming into our land. Famine has occurred before and it lasted several years. Many in our village are putting away hay and grains in case we need extra.

We say goodbye to each other. I watch my friend get smaller in the distance until I can no longer make out his figure. I hope to see my friend again. I turn to go and meet up with Abdon.

> [12] *And as he entered into a certain village, there met him ten men that were lepers, which stood afar off:* [13] *And they lifted up their voices, and said, Jesus, Master, have mercy on us.* [14] *And when he saw them, he said unto them, go shew yourselves unto the priests. And it came to pass, that, as they*

went, they were cleansed. ¹⁵ And one of them,
when he saw that he was healed, turned
back, and with a loud voice glorified God, ¹⁶
And fell down on his face at his feet, giving
him thanks: and he was a Samaritan. ¹⁷ And
Jesus answering said, were there not ten
cleansed? But where are the nine? ¹⁸ There
are not found that returned to give glory to
God, save this stranger. ¹⁹ And he said unto
him, Arise, go thy way: thy faith hath made
thee whole. (Luke 17:12-19) (KJV)

I am waiting for Abdon to meet up with me. We are
going to the market. As I am waiting, a small group of
people makes its way down the street. They hang behind
another group of people. Those walking in the street
sidestep around this small group. Some in the street stoop
to pick up rocks and cast them towards the small group.
It is only when they pass close by to me that I notice the
sores and smells of this small group. They are lepers and
have been living in the leper caves outside the city. One
of the men in the larger group turns his head and notices
the smaller group. Someone yells out in the crowd and
the small group fits together more closely but continues
to follow the larger group. I notice a familiar shape in the
larger crowd. He turns and says something to the small
group. In unison they turn and begin to make their way
down the street.

After several minutes one member of the small group
returns. He makes his way into the larger group. After
several moments he exits and makes his way down the
street. I notice that he appears clean and whole. Joy has

lightened his face. Several people in the large group turn back around and once again make their way up the street. Mary's son is the only one that hangs back from the main group. As I lean against the wall we notice each other, he nods his head towards me and I wave back. He beckons me with a wave of his hand to follow but I yell back "next time!" He then turns and catches up with his group. As this is happening Abdon has finally caught up to me against the wall. He has told me that he has something special planned for our day.

SIXTEEN

³⁵ And it came to pass, that as he was come nigh unto Jericho, a certain blind man sat by the way side begging: ³⁶ And hearing the multitude pass by, he asked what it meant. ³⁷ And they told him, that Jesus of Nazareth passeth by. ³⁸ And he cried, saying, Jesus, thou son of David, have mercy on me. ³⁹ And they which went before rebuked him, that he should hold his peace: but he cried so much the more, Thou son of David, have mercy on me. ⁴⁰ And Jesus stood, and commanded him to be brought unto him. (Luke 18:35-40) (KJV)

⁴² And Jesus said unto him, receive thy sight: thy faith hath saved thee. ⁴³ And immediately he received his sight, and followed him, glorifying God: and all the people, when they saw it, gave praise unto God. (Luke 18:42-43) (KJV)

I begin making my way down the street towards Abdon's house and am caught up with a group of people. Along the side of the road a blind man usually sits and begs for whatever scraps he can. On this particular day, as our group approaches he calls out in a loud voice, many in the crowd try to silence him but he cries out louder. Mary's son is in the middle of this group and hears the man cry out. He stops and says something to the man and the man immediately gets up and praises God. Unbelievable. This man sat by this road for years begging. Now he can see. Mary's son glances my way and beckons me with a wave of his hand to follow but I yell back "next time!"

And when he thus had spoken, he cried with a loud voice, Lazarus, come forth. *(John 11:43) (KJV)*

I am on my way to Bethany a small town several miles from my own. I follow a small group. Our journey will take several hours. As I near Bethany our small group has grown. Many people are standing along the road talking about the recent death of Lazarus.

As I near the house, moans and wails can be heard coming from the house. The group surrounding the house absorbs the group I started walking with. Several people in the crowd are moaning and wailing. Some of these people have been paid to wail. This group forms a line that the crowd passes on its way to the tomb.

Lazarus was well liked and was a true friend to many in his village. I see several women enter and exit the house bearing large baskets and jugs. It has been almost a week since the death of Lazarus. His body preparation and burial has already occurred several days ago. Some in the crowd have just recently heard about his death and have come to show the family that he will be greatly missed.

I begin to weave within the crowd; as I do this, the group collectively moves along the road. We continue for several minutes and then the group stops. I look over the heads of the group and notice that in front of us are tombs in the hills. We have arrived at the tomb of Lazarus and stand in front of the great stone entrance.

The crowd slowly parts and Mary's son appears along with a few of his group. The sisters of Lazarus are speaking to the small group and a look of concern crosses their faces. After a few moments Mary's son with a loud powerful voice commands Lazarus to come out. There are some Synagogue elders in the crowd and they are heard yelling angrily to him. Incredibly the large stone is rolled from the entrance. It's as if unseen hands have moved the great stone. No one is present but the great stone is simply rolled away from the entrance.

It is a breezy day and the smell of death issues from the tomb. It has been very warm for the past several weeks and the effects can be smelled from the tomb. After several more moments shrieks and cries can be heard from the crowd. As one we are moved several feet backward as a draped figure steps from the tomb. The crowd is transfixed and is rendered quiet. A figure steps forward. Mary and Martha, the sisters of the deceased rush forward and begin to unwrap the bindings. Slowly the hair and head can be seen. He is whole. He has been restored. A joyous cry issues from the crowd. Mary's son and his group turn to walk toward the house and enter closely followed by Mary, Martha and Lazarus.

I am confused. The paid mourners have become silent, unsure of what to do. Some turn away to begin their walk home. I begin to make my way back to my village. I cannot think or speak. As I walk, I catch comments floating on the air but I am stunned by what I have seen.

The preparation and burial had taken place. He had been buried for several days. The burial ceremony had already taken place. Several of the Synagogue elders participated in his ceremony and burial. I had only heard about his death a day ago. My parents urged me immediately to go. No one will believe me when I tell them what has occurred. I try to think of how to tell what I have seen and even I am too stunned to believe it. I remain stunned throughout my journey back home. As I approach, Abdon meets me. I try to tell him what I have seen and he scoffs at me and tells me of his plans for us today. Soon I am caught up in the plan he has for us. All thoughts of what I have seen are soon forgotten.

SEVENTEEN

45 And he went into the Temple, and began to cast out them that sold therein, and them that bought; 46 Saying unto them, It is written, My house is the house of prayer: but ye have made it a den of thieves. (Luke 19:45-46) (KJV)

My father, older brother and I are waiting to enter the Synagogue. Various merchants have set up their tables with their goods on them. They charge high prices for their goods but people often pay the higher price to obtain their sacrifice for the Synagogue. I am reminded of a memory in which several merchants lost their caged birds. A smile floats across my face thinking back and remembering the confusion that was caused by the flock escaping into the sky.

Today is warm and extremely bright in the courtyard of the Synagogue. I notice a now familiar small group enter and make their way up the stairs of the courtyard. I see a recognizable shape emerge from the group and he begins to immediately upend the merchant tables and their goods. Mary's son has made a small whip of twine and is casting it about wildly and yelling. The Pharisees are becoming angry and try to stop the situation. The men are afraid to get around the swinging whip. After a short time, the commotion stops and the group heads into the Synagogue.

The elders continue to loudly whisper about the destruction of the merchant items. The merchants are angry and much commotion is still heard outside the doors. Merchants want to know who is going to pay for the damages that were done. Several of the merchants corner some of the temple elders and try to get payment for what they lost.

The elders and some merchants look towards Mary's son and cast angry stares at him. He ignores them and begins to teach on forgiveness. The incident outside is soon forgotten as all listen to the teaching inside the temple. The elders also seem to have forgotten the incident at least for a while.

Our small village road takes us past where the Romans crucify the criminals. Abdon has grown fond of throwing small rocks and pebbles at those hanging on their cross. The dirt and rocks get lodged into the skin and dripping blood and I am sure only add more to their discomfort. Abdon has taken an immense liking to his hobby. The moans and cries of those hanging do not seem to affect him. In a coherent moment, one of the doomed men looks down on Abdon and says he hopes that he doesn't ever know what it is like to be hanged. Little do we know that is exactly what will happen to us in the future.

One of Abdon's favorite games has elicited my participation. We make our way up the hill and grab a handful of pebbles along the way. The feet and knees of those hanging from the crosses come into view. This was a special hanging. These recipients weren't Jewish, if they were Jewish, custom would mandate that they were to be removed before sundown. It has been over a day since this group was hung. Some of them are still alive. I can hear their moans and whimpers. Several have asked for water.

After gathering a handful of small pebbles, we take careful aim and let our grip of pebbles fly. Abdon laughs especially hard and his eyes glimmer in a way new to me. I am thinking how horrible and mean it was to add to those suffering up on the crosses. I drop my small collection of pebbles. Abdon says that if they hadn't done something really bad then they wouldn't be up on the cross. And that our throwing pebbles wouldn't add to the pain they were already in. The moans from those hanging will never leave me and I can still hear them. I will remember this episode later when I will face the same fate.

EIGHTEEN

Jerusalem is made up of several small villages all connected by a series of roads. Each village is protected by its own wall and gated entry with a small water supply for each town. Each individual town has its own upper and lower part. The rich and political live in the upper and nicest part of each town while the working class and those less fortunate live in the lower part.

I have been asked by my mother to help my sister with getting the large water jug filled. As I make my way to the well I pass by several women who attended the wedding in Cana. There are more already at the well and we all exchange greetings. These women also attended the wedding in Cana a very long time ago. After they have drawn their water, I assist my sister with our jug. The women who haven't left stand to the side and bits of their conversations float by me. If I hadn't been a witness to many of these events I would assume these women were making up some fantastic stories. In order to try to hear more, I angled my body towards the edge of the well closest to the women. They were too animated in their discussion to notice me. The move didn't bring me any better advantage. I still could only hear bits and pieces of what they were saying. Still, if I hadn't been a witness to many of these, I would think the stories were made up. The more outspoken woman repeated her story to the others. Amid gasps and cries of unbelief she repeated her story... *men brought in a bed with a man who couldn't walk: and after he had spoken to him the man got up and walked!...* and ... *he said unto the man, stretch forth thy hand. And he did so: and his hand was restored whole as the other ...* Still the one story that brought the more vivid response was ... *he said, arise and he that was dead sat up...*the women cried and gestured wildly. They asked more questions of the woman telling the story but I could not hear because of the noise my jug made returning from the depth of the well.

Abdon and his family are eating their meal. After the meal Abdon waits till the remains of the meal are cleared and the room put in order. He waits for one of the female servants to have her hands full and slips up behind her. He places his hands around her throat and slowly begins to squeeze. After several moments it begins to become difficult for her to breathe and she begins to struggle. This only causes Abdon to squeeze harder. She drops what she is carrying and begins to claw at his hands. She manages to claw his fingers from around her throat. Abdon somehow places his fingers over her mouth to keep her from screaming. She bites down hard on his fingers and causes him to release his grip. But the short interlude only fuels his anger more deeply and he again lunges for her. After several moments of struggling she is able to break free and a small scream escapes out of her mouth. Abdon's older sister is just returning to the house and hearing the servant scream, she makes her way inside the room and finds Abdon struggling with the servant. Abdon's sister manages to break them apart and the servant escapes to another part of the house. Abdon makes his way to his room vowing to finish what he started. He vows revenge.

It has been several months since the episode with the servant. Abdon's family is sitting down to their meal when his father notices that the usual female servant is missing. After the meal is complete, he issues a search of the house and grounds for the missing servant. After all rooms of the house are searched a search of the outside buildings is made. A male servant runs up to Abdon's father and gasping for air claims that the female servant has been found but that she is dead. Abdon's sister looks at him with a knowing glance. Abdon just remains silent with a smirk on his face.

After this incident most of the servants give a wide berth to Abdon when he is close by. A short time later, the female servant is replaced with a male servant and no other episodes occur at his house.

Whispers about the incident remain throughout the village. I have heard these rumors about Abdon, but in all my daily outings with him he has never shown me this side. The only time I remember him being bad to an animal was the fly incident. If you want to count the incident with the muddy goats then all right two times he was mean to animals. Although I tried to make known his good side, the rumors remain about him. These rumors are not nice; in fact they are downright hideous. Some rumors relate about his bullying the kids surrounding his house, some about his treatment of servants, and some about missing and dead animals. As much as I try to show Abdon in a good light the rumors remain and nothing I can say will turn the ideas about him.

NINETEEN

Later today I am to meet up with Abdon. Today he has another plan in mind to extract some money from an unsuspecting traveler. Before I meet up with him, I make my way to the Synagogue to discuss with the elders all the things I've seen. I begin to tell them of the many miraculous healings. They are able to answer me on how some of these things were done. I feel unsatisfied with their explanations and tell them of the child that was raised from the dead. They begin to become extremely animated in our discussion. I tell them that the whole town knew the child was dead and had been for a number of days. The body had been prepared for its first burial and given its bath of purity called tahara. It was after this had been done and while moving it to its resting place that the child was raised. The elders become angry with me when at every opportunity I counter their answers with what I have seen. One by one they dismiss me and make their way to some other part of the Synagogue. After the final elder has left I turn to go to meet up with Abdon. I see him making his way up the road and I begin to run to catch up to him. The answers the elders have given me are weighing heavily on my mind. I am still left with more questions than answers. I can't shake the image of several things that I have seen and heard. The elders were not present nor did they see what I saw. After my attempts at a discussion with the elders they turned their anger towards me. I try again to bring them into a discussion about all that I have seen but they refuse and become angrier with me. At this point I drop the discussion and turn to go. The lack of answers has left me empty and seeking answers.

TWENTY

We are hiding behind a large pile of boulders waiting for the sun to drop just a little more. Our plan is simple, and as we have done in the past, easy. Our target will be a single male making his way by foot. His moneybag will be full. We spy our target, a rather fat man with several bags hanging from the outside of his belt. Abdon prepares his knife to make extraction of the leather bags easier, the blade looks familiar to me, in fact it is the same blade I saw him purchase so long ago in the market.

I prepare to receive the hand-off. Our target is almost upon us. We both failed to see the small group of Roman soldiers following him in the distance. Abdon pounces on the target; Abdon has hit him several times about the head with a rock. A multitude of effects occurred from this but they all contributed to the final outcome. His screams have alerted the Roman group behind our target and causes them to run. Our target has put up a good fight. Suddenly, my arms are pulled awkwardly behind my back and I am pulled away and surrounded by three large and well-armed Roman guards. I yell to Abdon but for the moment he continues his assault. A few moments pass and he too is pulled off the target.

The target isn't moving or thrashing around like the others, in fact he lays eerily still. The small group of Roman soldiers is huddled around him wildly gesturing, some words are floating by on the air. Beaten, bloody, dead are the words I hear. It is then that the group looks toward Abdon and me. They tie our hands together and affix ropes to our waists so that we cannot run off.

Three guards stay in front of us and three guards trail behind us. We are securely fixed in our ropes and the thought of escape doesn't cross my mind. We are led away and cross in front of our victim. Abdon glances at him and glares. He remains motionless. I try to look more closely at his face and I do not recognize him he is a stranger to me.

TWENTY ONE

12 ... and he was numbered with the transgressors; (Isaiah 53:12) (KJV)

We are being led to the chief Roman magistrate for a quick trial. Guilty and death are the only words I hear. I am scared. I am very scared. Robbery and murder in the first century is punishable by death. A fact that Abdon and I knew but didn't think would happen to us, at least we didn't think very long or hard upon this fact. Our punishment will be quick. Jewish law dictates that killing and the burying of people occur outside a city. And executions must also take place outside the city gates.

The trial is short and quick. The Roman guards who happened upon the scene acted as witnesses to the outcome of our act. We will be scourged and then crucified. I become sick and vomit up what little remains in my stomach from my midday meal.

Only after hearing a deafening thwack does my mind register the pain. My failure to answer a question has bought my face a slap that radiates pain from my cheek along to my jaw line. A Roman guard has slapped me to get my attention.

I look over my right shoulder and I see Abdon, his head is hanging down and he refuses to look around. His father is doing a good job in arguing his case. I look over my left shoulder and see only my mother and siblings – weeping bitterly. Things are not looking good for me. I wonder "how did I end up here?" Our fate is quickly decided. We were caught in the act of robbery, which resulted in a death of a citizen and now we must die.

I guess you can say it started with the dirty goat incident but it ended horribly with the beating, robbery and death of a traveler. My earliest recollections seemed harmless but in looking back they seemed to escalate.

The Roman guards lead us away to be scourged. I remember in my youth, running by the hills and seeing the criminals hanging on crosses and hearing the yells and moans of those in the throes of death. I also remember throwing pebbles at some of the condemned. I remember thinking how grisly a death it is – the body suffocates and you very slowly succumb to death. Death is not quick and crucifixion was specifically designed and perfected as a very slow death.

We have been led to an interior courtyard for our scourging. Several guards and witnesses are permitted to watch the proceedings. Our garments are ripped from us and they lead us away to be tied to a large pole that has iron rings on either side so that our arms can be secured to the pole. The anticipation for the first strike of the whip is almost unbearable but nothing I have seen or heard has prepared me for the actual pain from the whip.

I have been stripped of my clothing except for a loincloth and my hands have been tied to a post. A Roman guard has stepped forward with the whip in his hand. Not an ordinary whip but one made special just for scourging, it has several leather thongs with small balls of lead attached near the ends of each throng. The whip is brought down with full force again and again across my shoulders, back, and legs. At first the weighted balls cut through my skin. The small balls of lead produce large deep bruises that are broken open by subsequent blows. I lose count and I fall unconscious.

I cannot be certain how long I was unconscious. When I awaken, the blows continue, they cut deeper. I cannot begin to describe the pain. I can hear my screams at each impact of the whip. I am grateful when the whippings stops and begin to cry.

TWENTY TWO

After the scourging we are led away to our final destination to be crucified. We have both been given the crossbeams of our individual crosses. We will be made to walk the distance to the same hill that I remember as a small boy, in my youth mocking and throwing pebbles to those hanging. The irony has not been lost on me.

Along the way it seems our entire village has come out to witness our trial and death. We make our way to the hill. I see three posts standing and waiting for us. I wonder whom the third beam has been reserved for. We are led to our individual posts. Abdon will be hung to the left of me. The one in the center remains empty for the time being but I notice in the distance that our other companion is slowly making his way to the site. It appears that the entire village has come out to see the man make his walk to the hill.

A small container bearing the nails is set down before me. Only these are not just simple nails but long and gruesome nails made special for this type of work. These nails are about one inch square on four sides and about seven inches long. The edges are extremely razor sharp. In earlier days I can recall the screams at each strike. I feel faint and quite sick. The guard picks up the hammer and a couple of nails and begins to make his way towards me. If I had not been restrained by several guards I would have turned and run away. I am being lowered to the ground. More like thrown to the ground. I am laid next to my cross. Gentleness is not part of the program for today. My arms and legs are being held in place by several guards. I watch as if in slow motion as the guard raises his hand with the hammer. Searing and excruciating pain radiates from my feet to my brain. With each pound of the hammer fresh new pain makes its way up my body. It becomes too much to bear but unlike the scourging I remain awake for each strike. It makes the scourging I received earlier pale in comparison to the pain I now experience. The pain seems unending and I scream. Finally the hammering stops and my post is raised.

After I am raised I can see all those below me and the surrounding countryside. I look down and can see several young boys playing and running. Their parents are somewhere in the crowd. One of the boys grabs a handful of rocks and throws them at Abdon who in turn screams. I am reminded of the time that Abdon and I did the same thing to a condemned man many years ago. The boy's father strides over angrily and grabs his son turning him away. I hear a little of what was said to the boy. The boy begins to cry in response.

It is time for Abdon to be secured to his post. Abdon is trying to talk the guards into knocking him out before they strike the nails. They laugh at him. The Roman guards ignore Abdon's request and begin to affix Abdon to his post. They are enjoying their task. Several of the guards speak to Abdon. It appears that some have instructed Abdon in the art of crucifixion. It is only when they begin that his screams resonate throughout the hill. They finish affixing him to his cross and begin to raise him. Now all must wait for our final breaths.

TWENTY THREE

It is extremely hard to breathe. Every breath brings fresh pain. Each exhale makes you want to take a deeper breath the next time. It is a slow and agonizing pain. As I inhale, my body moves slightly and the pain from my back and the open flesh exposed brings in more excruciating pain.

A small crowd has gathered before us. Abdon's father reaches out to him only to be struck away by a Roman guard. He turns and walks away, I see him make his way off the hill leaving Abdon to face his fate by himself. I look towards my mother and siblings, they continue to cry bitterly, I try to calm them but they cry harder. Nothing I say comforts them.

Our third companion is finally being raised up and I notice that it is Mary's son. I wonder what he has done to deserve such a harsh punishment. He is in far worse shape than either Abdon or myself, but I cannot imagine what he has done to receive such harsh treatment. His flesh hangs from his body and his face is almost unrecognizable. His body is caked with fluids. His scourging and beating was much worse when compared to ours.

I remember when he taught in the Synagogue and to the groups, and certainly nothing that I can recall that would elicit such a harsh punishment. It is only later as I hang on my cross that I realize the masses of people are crying for Him.

My memories of him began when I was much younger. I remember him reading from the scrolls in the temple and having fiery and deep discussions with the elders. I remember the elders saying his knowledge of the laws was remarkable especially in one so young and whose father was just a carpenter. I often heard the elders commenting on how he learned so much since his father could barely read himself. They often wondered where he learned and gained his knowledge. They settled on themselves that it was his mother who taught him his theories and how to read the laws.

It is now apparent that the elders were very jealous of him. Their jealousy was more of an intense hatred that would surface when Jesus would openly contradict what was written or taught by the elders. So extreme was their jealousy that when he would heal someone before them, the elders would become very angry. He was older at this time.

I remember several times of his healing those who were crippled or had some sickness. I remember him healing the lepers and also of him raising a person from being dead. I think surely this is not the reason why he is hung like a common criminal. I deserve my punishment but not Him. In my mind I recall all the times I was witness to the many great things that He did. He healed many, provided food to hundreds and thousands, he was able to raise back to life an only child to his mother, surely it was not due to these acts that he has been sentenced to our fate. His wounds appear worse than what we received. His body is a mess, the effects of the scourging he received is shown on every part of his body. Unlike Abdon and me, they have removed all his clothing and the guards are playing dice for the choicest pieces.

To try and take my mind off the pain, I scan the horizon. I notice some familiar faces in the crowd; they number quite a few. I see the woman whose arm Jesus restored, and I see the leper who was cleansed, and I see several of the blind men who can now see. A cluster of people has made its way up the hill. A face in the group is recognizable. In fact, I believe it is the man who was lowered from the roof so long ago and was healed. He approaches Jesus and bows his head and knee. The crowd grows quiet. After he rises he makes his way back down the hill. Another group is making their way to see Jesus.

A small group attended by a few women follows this man. The elders try to block his path but he scowls and says something and the elders allow him to pass. The crowd remains quiet and a few gasps are heard. The man who approaches is named Lazarus. Many years ago Jesus visited his village to visit his friend who had died only now he is alive. The elders again try to block his path and they try to speak to the crowd but the crowd throws rocks at the elders. There are several others but the effects of my scourging is is getting into my eyes and it is making it difficult to see.

Several of the temple elders are yelling to those who have made their way up to see Jesus. Some begin to leave but others remain. Those who remain are the ones healed by Jesus. After several attempts of trying to get the crowd to leave the elders turn and begin mocking Jesus. Abdon adds his voice. I begin to yell at Abdon and the elders to stop their harassment.

I try to comfort my family while Abdon continues to taunt several onlookers in the crowd. I yell at him to stop and he focuses his gaze at me. I am in too much pain to let any feelings I have get in the way and I yell back at him. He stops yelling but remains defiant and continues to glare at everyone.

TWENTY FOUR

> [39] And one of the malefactors which were hanged railed on him, saying, If thou be Christ, save thyself and us. [40] But the other answering rebuked him, saying, Dost not thou fear God, seeing thou art in the same condemnation? [41] And we indeed justly; for we receive the due reward of our deeds: but this man hath done nothing amiss. [42] And he said unto Jesus, Lord, remember me when thou comest into thy kingdom. [43] And Jesus said unto him, Verily I say unto thee, To day shalt thou be with me in paradise. (*Luke 23:39-43) (KJV)*

I am very scared. A very real fear grips me with new pain. This pain is not physical even though the physical pain remains. This pain or I should say fear is every bit as real. This fear has taken hold of me. It grips me in a very real way. The fear is the not knowing what will happen to me when I die. I have been taught that because I am Jewish I will meet father Abraham, Moses and God. I will not suffer anymore and that for all eternity I will enjoy heaven. For as much as was taught in my daily instruction, I still feel unsure. For many years I have been told that because we are God's chosen people we will see heaven. But I am still unsure. I try to remember my lessons and am still uneasy of the next phase. Throughout my study at the Synagogue I did not pay much attention when they taught on the subject of the afterlife. I did not feel it necessary because the elders taught that our eternity as a chosen people was assured. My mind would often wander to what I was going to be doing after my daily studies were concluded. I remember sitting in Synagogue but falling asleep when this particular topic came up. As I ponder some of my past actions I feel that I really wasn't all that bad a person and none of the episodes really harmed anyone.

Except for some materials and time I can't recall a single person getting physically hurt. But I am still afraid. I wish I had paid more attention. Some of what Jesus talked about came to my mind. I remember sitting in the Synagogue waiting for Abdon. Jesus was sitting in the front in discussion with the elders. They were focused intently on their discussion. Jesus was saying that if anyone looks on Him they have seen God. Well, this really set off the elders and many cursed and spit and tore their clothes. Jesus continued and ignored them saying that if you believed in Him you will be saved and enter into heaven. This comment was just too much and really sent the elders over the edge. And finally when I thought nothing could top their discussion, Jesus laid claim to having the ability to sit at the right hand of God. At this, several of the elders became very red in the face and several left. Others appeared that at any moment they might fall over.

When I left the Synagogue, I looked over my shoulder and saw Jesus still in active debate. I was too far away and could not hear the rest of their discussion. But judging from the gestures of some of the elders it was not a friendly discussion.

I will be dead soon. I am struck by all the images from my past. All the chances that I did not act upon, chances I was given in seeing what Jesus did. He is who he says he is. Only God could do the things he did. These memories slam into my thinking in such a way that it leaves me breathless. As I ponder this Abdon curses and rails at Jesus. In my short life I can count the times I have directed my anger at Abdon. This is one of those times.

I am brought back to my current state when the post I am nailed on is shaken slightly. Abdon continues to hurl insults and some of the Synagogue elders make their way closer. They speak unkind words to Jesus and Abdon joins in with his mockery. I have had enough and I scream at him. 'I was stupid to follow after you. I look back at all the episodes that caused me trouble and they were from your hands.' 'Now look at us, we will be dead soon!' Abdon only glares at me while I scream at him. And although the physical pain does not go away, I feel slightly better that I can voice my anger at Abdon for if it weren't for him I would not be hanging on this pole.

As I begin to remember all the times I had to repair or replace items and contemplate the schemes that occurred I suddenly realize that I too am responsible for my current position. Had I been stronger, had I said no more often, had I just turned away and not taken part of the scheme, I may not have ended up here. Shame washes over me.

I turn to Jesus and he comforts me. Not only comforts me but my fear is completely gone. It has vanished. Only my physical pain remains.

Paradise. That word brings me great comfort. I am no longer afraid. One word. I look at Jesus and am amazed that he still lives. His skin is hanging off him. Blood and other fluids continue to ooze out of his body. But he continues to breathe. I see his mother and a man I recognize from his group. Even though their faces show signs of tears they are not crying now. I see several members of the elders from our temple. They approach Abdon and me. They begin to speak but their words are taken away by the howl of the wind. I continue to die. The pain, which never left, continues to assail me every time the wind blows and shakes my cross. It moves across my body and it leaves a trail of pain when it crosses over me. I try to focus on things other than the pain.

I again have flashbacks to memories of my youth. I see several neighbors in the crowd that I helped in my earlier days. One neighbor I helped when their door became unhinged, another whose roof needed some repair, another whose fence needed mending, I even notice the owner of the flock that Abdon and I disguised by coating the flock with dirt and mud.

I notice a few others that are standing near but are not crying. They stand in front of Abdon and yell up at him. An older man stands in front of the pole and shakes his fist at Abdon. Abdon yells back at the man and shows no remorse for what he did. Several others of his group begin to make their way closer and are stopped by a guard. I can only assume that these must be friends or family members of the man whose life we ended and with me nailed to this pole. How I would like to take back that day and how I would like to have been stronger against Abdon and his hold over me.

Abdon is returning insults to the crowd. There are several Jewish Synagogue leaders standing among the crowd but are only interested in Jesus. They linger with the rest of the crowd just waiting. The high priest approaches Jesus and again mocks him. The other temple leaders hang back and continue to watch the crowd.

I remember the times I was witness to several of his healings, the feeding of the people on the hill and even witness to the miracle of Him raising someone from the dead. Who else but God could do these signs and wonders? I also remember all the times He would invite me to join Him but there was always a 'next time.'

One of the Synagogue leaders approaches and begins to speak to Jesus. Abdon joins in with some harassing words. I have had enough. It is one of a few times where I stood against Abdon. I speak loudly against Abdon and he quiets down. I look towards Jesus and notice that His head is hung low and that he is barely breathing. Abdon begins a fresh onslaught of harassment. I have really had enough now and make it clear to Abdon to end his words, he looks at me with fresh contempt.

We have hung for hours. I guess the Romans are tired of waiting and try to hurry things along by using a dreadful technique called crurifracture. As if having nails nailed into your hands and feet and being hung is not bad enough, the guards begin to break our legs. We will be dead soon after this is done. The guard wielding this special club decides to start at Abdon's post. After taking careful aim he releases the club with all his strength and successfully breaks his legs. Abdon screams which seems to echo around the hill. The guard approaches Jesus but notices that he is already dead. It is now my turn. I brace myself for what comes next. But no matter what I do there is awful pain. My vision begins to blur and things begin to whirl past. I begin to lose conscience. I try my best to remain coherent but it becomes more difficult as the minutes pass. I pass out. When I regain thought it is short as I feel myself slipping away.

✝ TWENTY FIVE

My gaze floats across the onlookers and into the distance. I notice a lone figure standing on a far off hill, tending sheep. My mind may be playing tricks on me but I would like to believe it is my father.

The individual raises his staff. My hands are secured to this pole and I am prohibited from returning his wave. I again look down on my family. It is getting very cold. I begin to shiver uncontrollably. I no longer feel pain. In fact I am quite numb. I am only feeling cold as the wind circles around the hill.

Although the day has darkened, and I feel my life ending, I am calm. My comfort rests in the assurance that I have somehow escaped the clutches of hell and will walk in heaven. Jesus has promised me paradise. I am assured what he has told me is truth.

My thoughts turn to Abdon who still remains defiant and continues to sling insults at the crowd. I turn my eyes toward my mother and family and to the neighbors whom I assisted before my actions took me down another path.

I think about all these things and to the times when I was witness to the many miracles that Jesus performed. I try to form words of comfort to my family but only a breathy whisper escapes my mouth.